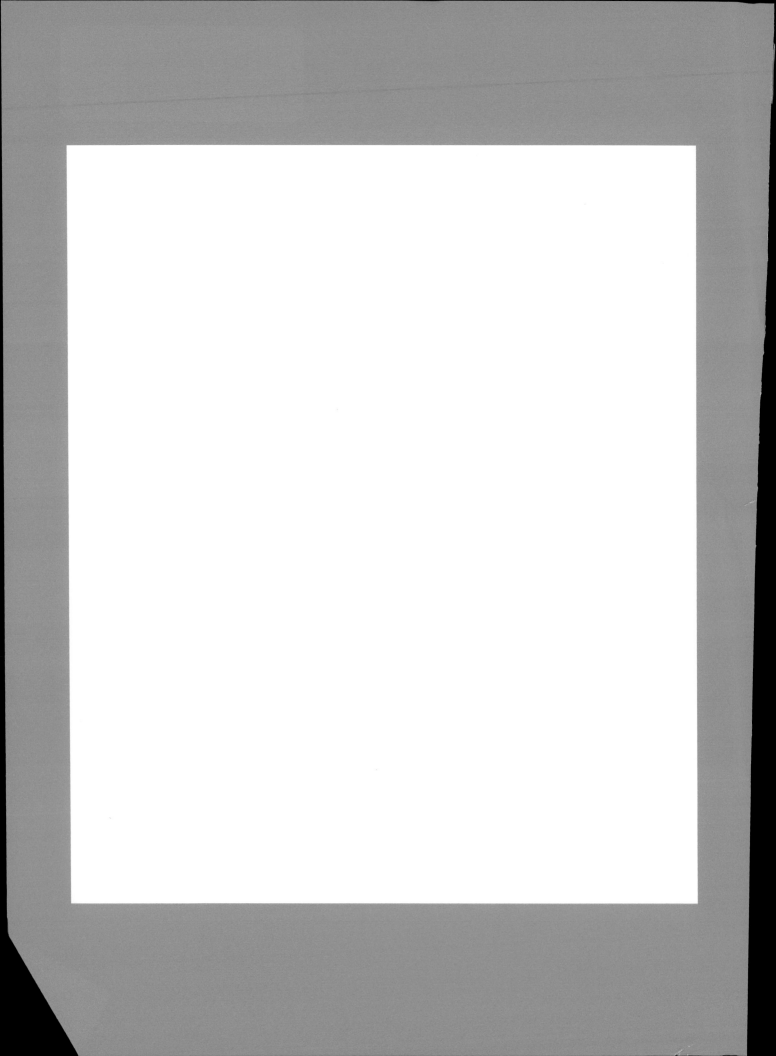

Schmoo Tales

Schmoo *Loves* Florida Life

Written and Illustrated by

Cheryl G. Kaye

Schmoo Tales
Schmoo *Loves* ***Florida Life***

This is a work of imagination. Any similarities to real doggies are used intentionally by Schmoo, the Jack Russell Terrier.

The illustrations in this book represent scrapbook pages from Schmoo's life. They are mixed-media images created by Cheryl G. Kaye.   Children can find Schmoo's signature pawprints hidden in the illustrations. The pawprints on the bottoms of pages and the back cover photograph by kwadrat70 are licensed from Adobe photostock.

ISBN: 9798542128559

Dedication and Acknowledgements

I lovingly dedicate this book to my grandchildren and children of all ages. As they read about Schmoo's animated, comical adventures, I hope they delight in her silly experiences as much as Schmoo enjoyed reliving and sharing them. Our little, spotted Jack Russell Terrier is loved by everyone who meets her.

I would like to sincerely thank and dedicate this book to Mary Reynolds for her insight and belief in making Schmoo be the best that she could be. She is my friend, my book designer and editor. She is also a talented artist, painter, and author of children's books. Together we edited Schmoo's words and adventures. We are both members of the Plantation Writers Guild in Leesburg, Florida. Mary gave me the courage and incentive to create my own whimsical illustrations. Thanks to her confidence in me, we created two of Schmoo's books together: Schmoo Moves to Florida and Schmoo Loves Florida Life.

The Tooth Fairy Visits Schmoo was retold (with Schmoo's help) and written by my identical twin sister, Michelle Ritson. She cleverly developed Schmoo's rhythmic tale in about thirty minutes!

Table of Contents

Schmoo *Loves* Florida Life

Schmoo's First Christmas...............8

Schmoo's Easter Bunny...................28

Schmoo Goes Shopping...................41

My Mom and Me....................................53

The Tooth Fairy Visits Schmoo........65

A Year in the Life of Schmoo............73

Coming soon...*Schmoo's Calendar Year*

PARADISE FOUND

SPF 30

Schmoo's First Christmas

About three weeks before Christmas Day

　　as Mom turned over the calendar, I heard her say,

"It's December, my favorite time of year

　　to spread good wishes and lots of cheer."

My family brought home two tall, green trees,

one for each main room.

"Why are these trees now in our home?

They belong outside where I play and roam."

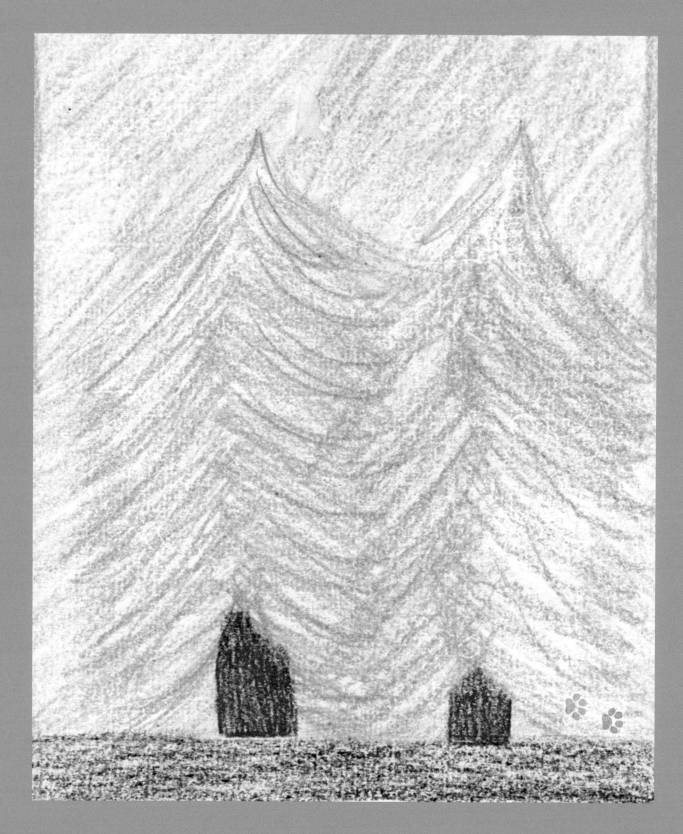

They decorated the trees with colorful lights,

along with ribbons and bows.

The shimmering tinsel hung so low

and tickled my little nose!

Soon cards were placed for all to see

upon a perfect shelf.

Of course I thought they all were mine

to rip up by myself.

"Oh, what fun, so much I see,

I bet my family did this for me!

So many pretty boxes placed under the trees,

sniff-sniff-sniff, what could they be?"

"Could there be a bone in there for me,

in that box, underneath that tree?

A cookie, a rawhide, a brand new sweater,

for me to wear out in cold weather?"

"Hmmm, let's see, I think I'll peek

into a box with my doggie beak.

I'll wait until there's no one home,

so I can explore these boxes alone."

One by one, I opened the gifts,

with oh such sheer delight!

I tossed wrapping paper here and there.

I tossed wrapping paper everywhere!

I finally found lots of doggie bones,

tucked in a great big box.

Along with a bright, red Christmas sweater,

that came with matching socks!

With my belly full of treats and stuff,

I finally felt like I'd had enough.

So I curled up in my doggie bed,

while visions of sweet treats danced
in my head.

Schmoo's Easter Bunny

It was almost dawn. I looked out at the lawn

and saw the strangest sight.

From my upstairs window, I watched in dim

light,

an odd-looking bunny that was *not* there

last night!

As fast as my short legs could carry me,
  I ran down the stairs so I could see,
    if my mom or dad would open my door.
I definitely wanted to see some more!

I pushed open my doggy door and ran outside.
It seemed odd, this huge bunny did *not* try to
    hide!
It did *not* try to run up the fence or a tree.
It fact, it wasn't even *afraid* of me!

I barked and I growled as I ran toward this bunny.
My parents laughed at me. They both thought it was
    funny.

'Cause upon the soft, young grass so green,
    stood the fattest bunny I'd ever seen!

It swayed in the breeze and was tied down by a rope.
It even looked friendly, which gave me some hope.

My mom said, "Oh, Schmoo, the bunny's not real.
Come over here. I'll let you feel
   the squishy, soft, air-filled bunny so tall
     just like the ones we saw at the mall!"

"Is it Easter, Mom? Is it Easter Sunday today?
Are the children coming here to find eggs and play?
Can I fill my basket with bones and my food?"
"Yes, Little Schmoo, and your friends can come, too!"

38

Happy Easter from Schmoo!

Schmoo Goes Shopping

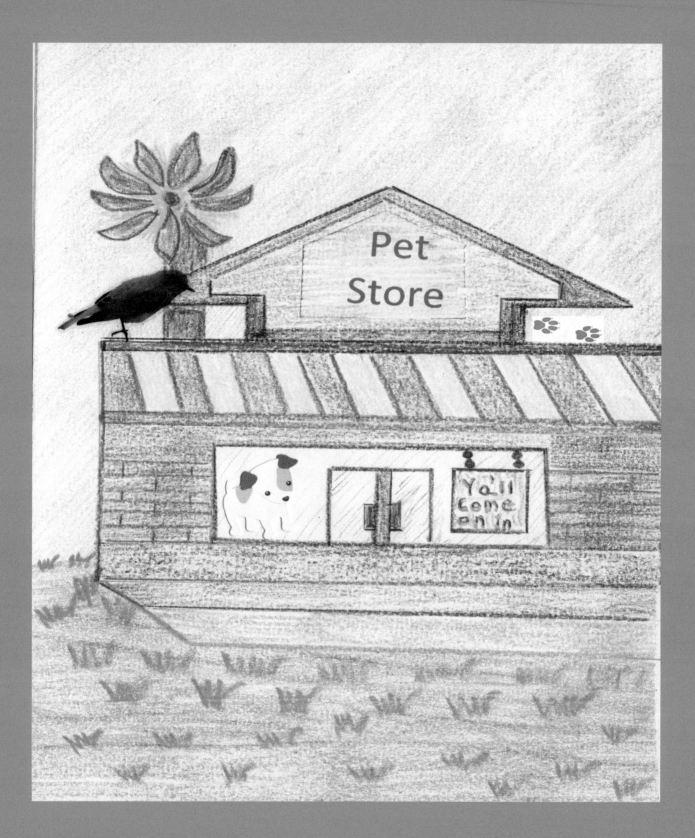

Schmoo went to a store with her friends.
The pet store sign said, "Ya'll come on in."

Schmoo tiptoed inside with eyes open wide,
not knowing just where to begin.

Schmoo walked on a lead with her master.
Schmoo was curious and wanted to walk faster.

Her mom told Schmoo, "No!
    You need to walk slow."
Schmoo's heart just might overflow!

Schmoo and her friends walked right in,
    with excitement and lots of huge grins.

They each wagged their tails, on the floor clicking
    nails.
Now their shopping fun soon would begin.

Schmoo knew just what she had come for.

She tip-toed toward the glass door.

The door held behind

   adoptees of all kinds.

Schmoo knew she wanted to do more.

Schmoo pushed her nose deep inside.
The solid glass door opened wide.

She let out a bark, saying, "Listen to me.
Let's open your cages so you can be free!"

"Hey, pups, come on over here.
The dog treats, snacks, and cookies are near.

The reds are beef-flavored and a few are lime green.
Each pup take a Greenie to keep your teeth clean!"

There were a few cats, but not many today.

They seemed happy resting, not wanting to play.

Schmoo's new friends were a ShiTzu and Doxie.

Their colorful scarves made them look really foxy!

Schmoo thought...

Will they have their own home one day?
A home where they're loved and could play?

A home where they're given some toys and a bed
  with a fluffy, warm blanket to cover their head?

Schmoo's mom said...

"Say goodbye to your friends till next week.
We'll come back and play hide-and-seek.

Ask your friends to go back behind the glass door.
    Of course we'll return and frolic some more."

Schmoo's friends said together...

"Thanks for a fun day, Schmoo. Come back soon!"

My Mom and Me

For five years, I've been an only child.

Most people call me "The Schmoo."

I've been the gleam in my mother's eyes.

My mom knows I love her, too!

For years it's been just her and me,
    I am her guiding light.

She rushes home from work to be
    close to me at night!

our paradise

She takes me everywhere she goes.

She dresses me up in pretty clothes.

She jingles her keys, and I run to the door.

We're going outside to play some more!

I love my mom. Her name is Amy.

I've always been her only baby.

Until one day my world got smaller.

She brought home a dog — a wee bit taller!

A brown, four-legged beagle hound
stumbled into my "space" one day.

Mom adopted her from a local pound.
Her name was Mattie Mae!

She ate my toys, tore them to shreds.

She even took over my mama's bed.

Oh, no, the drama does not stop here.
Mom brought home a baby the very next year.

A human baby that mom never let go.
Soon all I heard was, *"No, Schmoo-Moo, no!"*

Mom and dad named their baby Rae Helene.
Two happier parents I'd never seen.

They carried Little Rae both day and night.
They watched me carefully...*as if I would bite*!

Mattie Mae has become my fun friend.
The little human baby? Ah, well, I simply pretend.

I stay far away as she crawls toward my bones.
Both of my playmates won't leave me alone!

I know my mom. She still loves me to bits.
She kisses and hugs me when she finally sits!

Mom tells me that I will always be
     her first "baby girl."
               My Mom and Me!

The Tooth Fairy Visits Schmoo

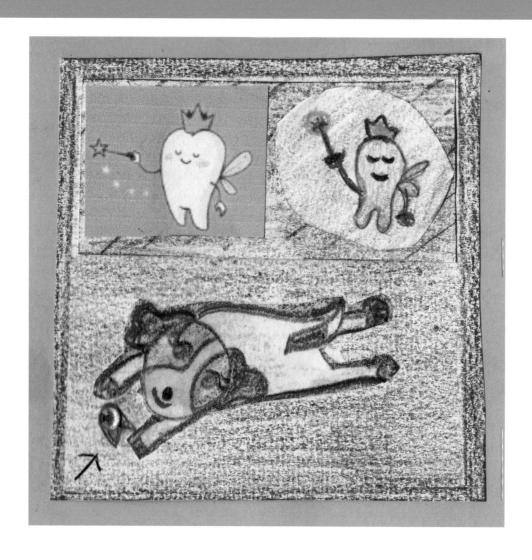

I remember being a little pup,

about the age of two.

I found my tooth lying at my side,

and I didn't know what to do.

I ran to the mirror to take a look

at the space now in my smile.

Getting used to my new look, I thought,

would certainly take a while.

**I held on to my tooth,
my newly found treasure.**

**I showed it to my mom,
who smiled at me with
pleasure.**

"You're growing up, my little pup,
   and I have a surprise for you.

It's a very special pillow
   from the tooth fairy to our Schmoo."

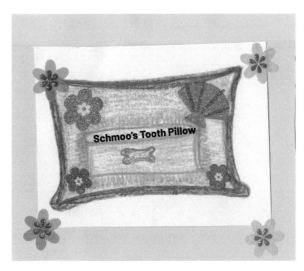

Schmoo's Tooth Pillow

That night when I was tucked into bed,
Mom put my tooth pillow under my head.
She said, "Go to sleep, and when you arise,
the tooth fairy will have visited,
leaving you a surprise."

"A prize that could be a small toy or yummy.
I'll hope for some carrots, dog cookies or gummies."

I tried to stay awake that night. I almost fell asleep.
But I heard tiny footsteps, so very close to me.

She fluttered and gently put a prize beneath my head.
Happiness was waking up in the morning, finding
     cookies in my bed!

Thank you, Tooth Fairy!

A Year in the Life of Schmoo

January is a favorite month for me.

Theme parks are empty. There's so much to see.

Pink flamingoes, Orca whales and porpoises share
their beautiful natural habitats so rare.

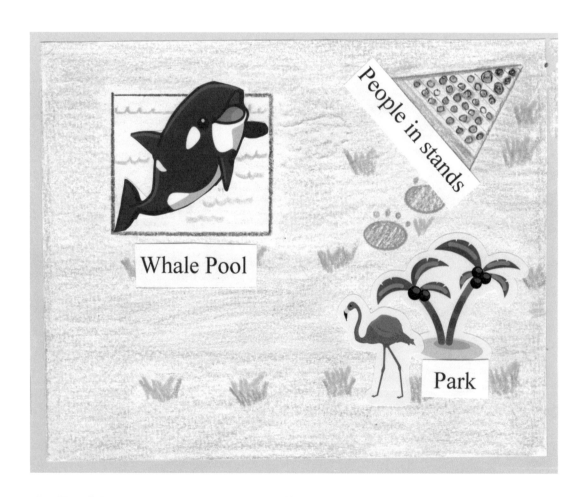

January

Sunday	Monday	Tuesday	Wednesday	Thursday	Friday	Saturday
						1 New Year's Day (US UK DE FR IT ES)
2	3	4	5	6	7	8
9	10	11	12	13	14	15
16	17 Martin Luther King, Jr. Day (US)	18	19	20	21	22
23	24	25	26	27	28	29
30	31					

In **February**, the weather's not much better.

I hardly ever take off my sweater.

So my friends and I relax in the sun
   feeling joy in the hearts of everyone.

February

Sunday	Monday	Tuesday	Wednesday	Thursday	Friday	Saturday
		1	2	3	4	5
6	7	8	9	10	11	12
13	14 Valentine's Day (US UK DE FR IT ES)	15	16	17	18	19
20	21 Presidents' Day (US)	22	23	24	25	26
27	28					

March days are warmer. They lead us to spring.

With trees and flowers, so many blooming things.

The short days of winter soon leave us behind.

Getting out of the house, I'm no longer confined.

March

Sunday	Monday	Tuesday	Wednesday	Thursday	Friday	Saturday
		1	2	3	4	5
			Ash Wednesday (US UK DE ES)			
6	7	8	9	10	11	12
13	14	15	16	17	18	19
Daylight Saving Time Begins (US)				St. Patrick's Day (US UK DE)		
20	21	22	23	24	25	26
First Day of Spring (US)						
27	28	29	30	31		

17 March
St Patrick's
DAY

April showers bring May flowers
and lots of sunny days.
I get to go outside a lot
to romp and roll and play.

April

Sunday	Monday	Tuesday	Wednesday	Thursday	Friday	Saturday
					1	2
3	4	5	6	7	8	9
10 Palm Sunday (US UK DE ES)	11	12	13	14	15 Good Friday (US UK DE FR IT ES) Passover, Begins at Sunset (US)	16
17 Easter (US UK DE FR IT ES)	18 Easter Monday (UK DE FR IT ES)	19	20	21	22 Earth Day (US UK DE FR IT ES)	23
24	25	26	27	28	29	30

In **May** we meet at the neighborhood park.

We go several times a week.

Mattie-Mae and I get to run, play, and bark.

We arrive after school and stay until dark.

May

Sunday	Monday	Tuesday	Wednesday	Thursday	Friday	Saturday
1	2 Labour Day (UK DE FR IT ES)	3	4	5	6	7
8	9 Mother's Day (US) WWII Victory Day (FR)	10	11	12	13	14
15	16	17	18	19	20	21
22	23	24	25	26	27	28
29	30 Memorial Day (US) Spring Bank Holiday (UK)	31				

In June, we spent fun-filled days at the shore.

I chased the sand pipers, sand crabs, and much
  more.

A beagle named Jack became my new buddy.

We chewed on driftwood, dug holes, and got muddy.

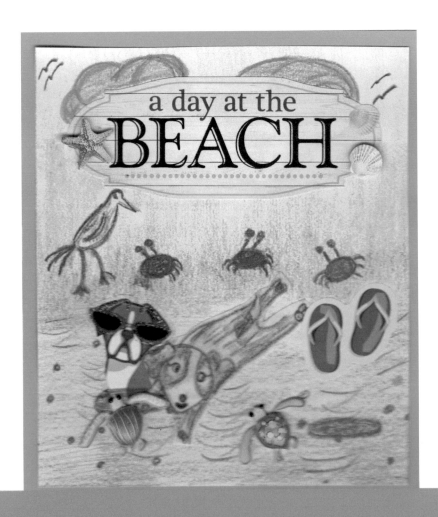

June

Sunday	Monday	Tuesday	Wednesday	Thursday	Friday	Saturday
			1	2	3	4
5	6	7	8	9	10	11
12	13	14 Flag Day (US)	15	16	17	18
19 Father's Day (US UK FR)	20	21 First Day of Summer (US)	22	23	24	25
26	27	28	29	30		

The July 4th fireworks light up the night sky.

We don't like the noises, so we run and hide.

We hide under blankets, pillows, and beds.

We bury ourselves and cover our heads.

July

Sunday	Monday	Tuesday	Wednesday	Thursday	Friday	Saturday
				1	2	3
4 Independence Day (US)	5	6	7	8	9	10
11	12	13	14	15	16	17
18	19	20	21	22	23	24
25	26	27	28	29	30	31

In **August**, the county fair comes to town.

The music, the rides and the merry-go-round
are all part of this wonderful week.

These memories I'll cherish and always keep.

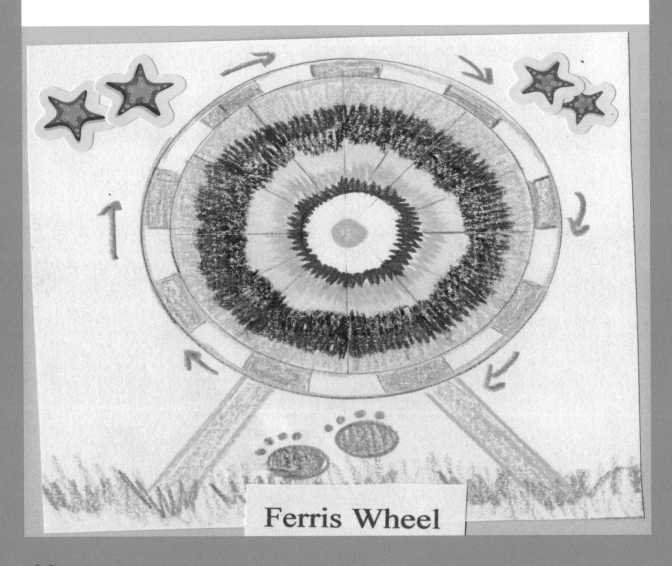

Ferris Wheel

August

Sunday	Monday	Tuesday	Wednesday	Thursday	Friday	Saturday
1	2	3	4	5	6	7
8	9	10	11	12	13	14
15	16	17	18	19	20	21
22	23	24	25	26	27	28
29	30	31				

September days bring the cool, light, fresh air.

We spend time outside and nap in mom's chair.

With my sister, Mattie-Mae and our kitten, Me-Me,
  we get up to eat dinner and return to our sleep.

September

Sunday	Monday	Tuesday	Wednesday	Thursday	Friday	Saturday
			1	2	3	4
5	6	7	8	9	10	11
	Labor Day (US) Rosh Hashanah, Begins at Sunset (US)					Patriot Day (US)
12	13	14	15	16	17	18
Grandparents Day (US)			Yom Kippur, Begins at Sunset (US)			
19	20	21	22	23	24	25
			First Day of Autumn (US)			
26	27	28	29	30		

Autumn's splendor, October is so gold
    with the smell of wood burning from chimneys
    and stoves.

New colors of reds, browns, and crisp greens
    give me energy to romp in dad's leaves.

October

Sunday	Monday	Tuesday	Wednesday	Thursday	Friday	Saturday
					1	2
3	4	5	6	7	8	9
10	11 Columbus Day (US)	12	13	14	15	16
17	18	19	20	21	22	23
24	25	26	27	28	29	30
31 Halloween (US UK DE)						

November is a time to give thanks on Thanksgiving.

It reminds me of how I'm blessed to be living
 in my forever home, no longer alone.

I now have love, friends, food, and chew bones.

November

Sunday	Monday	Tuesday	Wednesday	Thursday	Friday	Saturday
	1	2	3	4	5	6
		Election Day (US)				
7	8	9	10	11	12	13
Daylight Saving Time Ends (US)						
14	15	16	17	18	19	20
21	22	23	24	25	26	27
				Thanksgiving Day (US)		
28	29	30				
Hanukkah, Begins at Sunset (US)						

December is celebrated in many ways.

My family and I love fun-filled days.

Together we'll once again play in the sand,
listening to calpyso-style music
and kettle drum bands.

Merry Christmas!

Love,

Schmoo

December

Sunday	Monday	Tuesday	Wednesday	Thursday	Friday	Saturday
			1	2	3	4
5	6	7	8	9	10	11
12	13	14	15	16	17	18
19	20	21 First Day of Winter (US) December Solstice (UK DE FR IT ES)	22	23	24	25 Christmas Day (US UK DE FR IT ES)
26	27	28	29	30	31 New Year's Eve (US UK DE FR IT ES)	

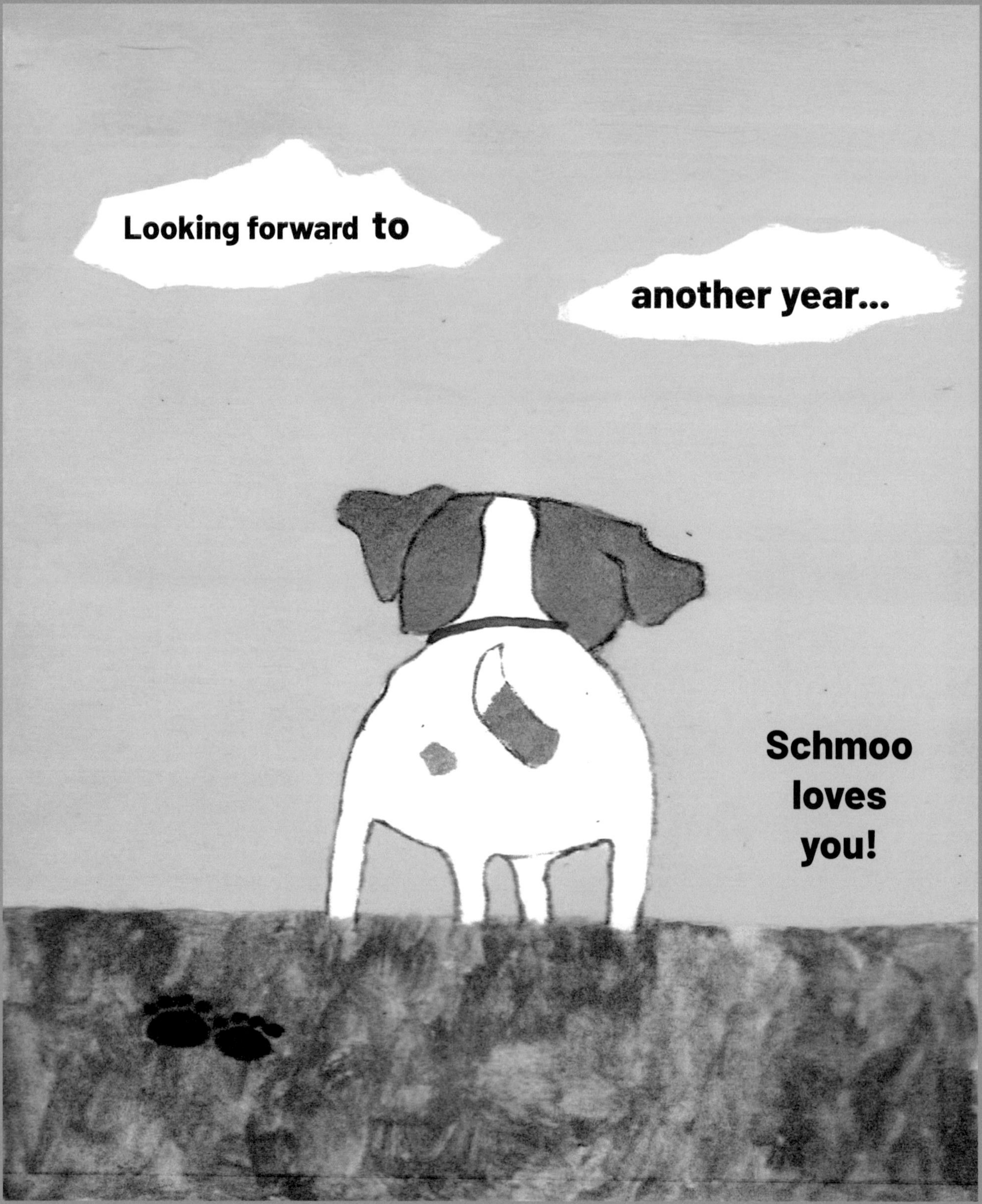
Looking forward to
another year...
Schmoo
loves
you!

About the Author/Illustrator

Cheryl G. Kaye

As a children's educator of literature, science, and reading for thirty-eight years, Cheryl G. Kaye has a remarkable gift for reaching the imagination of her readers.

Her goal as a reading teacher is to have emergent readers become independent readers for fun. Schmoo's stories engage a student's imagination through rhyme, rhythm, and playful illustrations. Come along on Schmoo's many adventures. You will fall in love with every story.

Made in the USA
Columbia, SC
18 November 2024

46565854R00058